D1303944

Coco's Surprise

For a free color catalog describing Gareth Stevens' list of high-quality books and multimedia programs, call 1-800-542-2595 (USA) or 1-800-461-9120 (Canada). Gareth Stevens Publishing's Fax: (414) 332-3567.

Library of Congress Cataloging-in-Publication Data available upon request from publisher.
Fax: (414) 332-3567 for the attention of the Publishing Records Department.

ISBN 0-8368-2731-7

This edition first published in 2000 by
Gareth Stevens Publishing
A World Almanac Education Group Company
330 West Olive Street, Suite 100
Milwaukee, WI 53212 USA

This edition © 2000 by Gareth Stevens, Inc. Original © 1998 by Uitgeverij J. H. Gottmer/
H. J. W. Becht bv, Haarlem, The Netherlands. Illustrations © Vera de Backker.
Text © Karen van Holst Pellekaan. Originally published under the title *Koosje is boos*.

English text by Jo Ann Early Macken.

Printed in the United States of America

1 2 3 4 5 6 7 8 9 04 03 02 01 00

Coco's Surprise

Illustrations by Vera de Backker
Written by Karen van Holst Pellekaan

Gareth Stevens Publishing
A WORLD ALMANAC EDUCATION GROUP COMPANY

Coco loves to crawl into the pouch on Mama's tummy. Coco is too big now for the pouch, but it's still the best place in the world.

Today Mama says, "No, Coco."

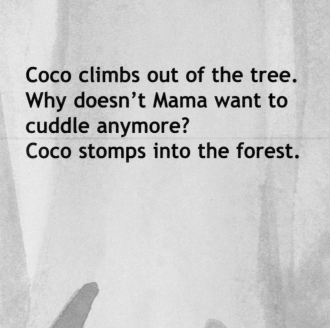

Coco climbs out of the tree.
Why doesn't Mama want to
cuddle anymore?
Coco stomps into the forest.

Hey, whose tail is that?

It's a kangaroo's tail. Shhh!
The kangaroo is asleep.

The kangaroo has a pouch, too.
Coco wonders if it is as soft
and warm as Mama's.

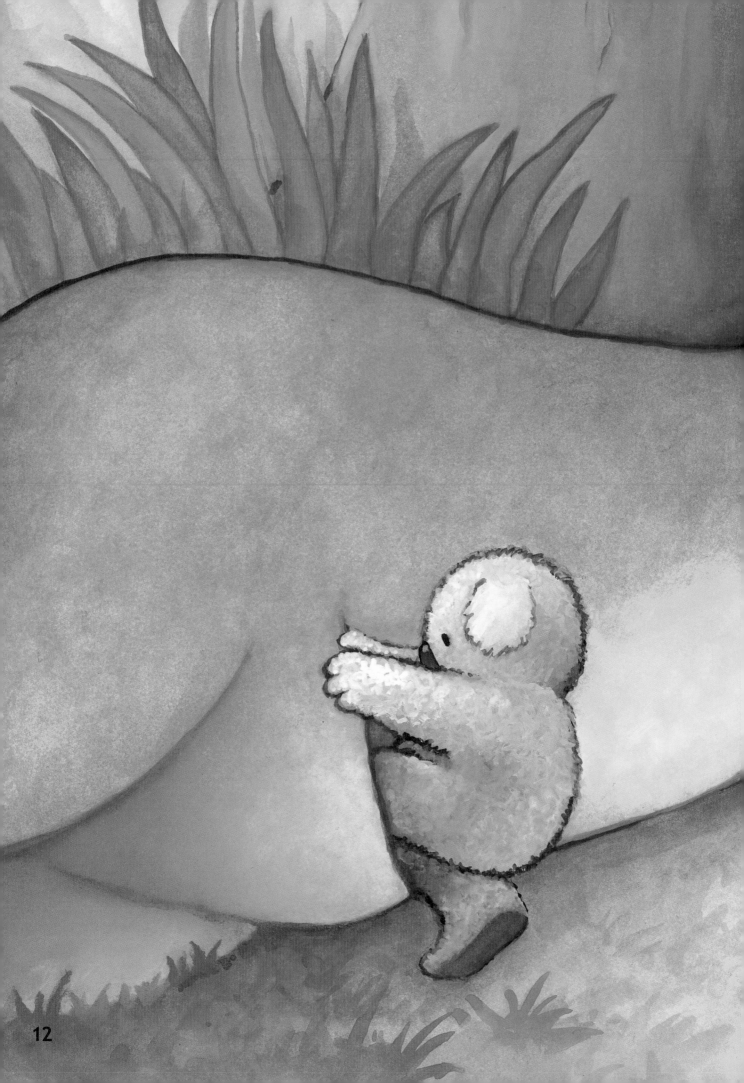

The kangaroo snores softly, and Coco
tiptoes — one, two, three — into the
pouch. What a wonderful place!
Coco curls up and falls asleep.

A little while later, the
kangaroo wakes up.
Its tummy is rumbling.
It's time for a snack.

Hop, hop, hop!
Suddenly, Coco wakes up.
What's going on?
What's shaking so much?
Where am I?

"Why are you in my pouch?"
asks the surprised kangaroo.
"I was just taking a nap,"
squeaks Coco.

"Where is your mama?" asks the kangaroo.
"I don't know," Coco replies.
"Who is she?"
"My mama is mean," grumbles Coco. "She won't
cuddle with me."
"Hmmm . . . mean. I think I know who your mama is."
Hop, hop, hop. They stop at a tree.

Coco is afraid.
"That scary animal isn't my mama!"
"Who is your mama, then?"
asks the kangaroo.
Coco thinks. "She never has time
for me," she says.
"Hmmm . . . busy, busy, busy.
I think I know who your mama is."

Hop, hop, hop. They stop at a bush.

MAMA?

20

Coco is confused.
"That busy creature isn't
my mama!"
"Who is your mama, then?"
asks the kangaroo.
"Lately, she complains a lot."
"Hmmm . . . grouchy.
I think I know who your mama is."

Hop, hop, hop.
They stop at an anthill.

MAMA?

Coco is annoyed.
"That prickly animal isn't
my mama!"
"Who is your mama, then?"
asks the kangaroo.
"She has very soft fur."
"Hmmm . . . soft. I think I know
who your mama is."

Hop, hop, hop. They stop at a river.

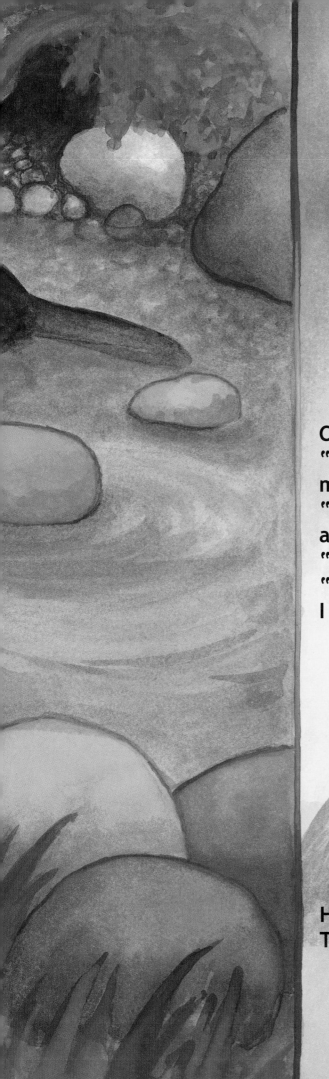

Coco is sad.
"That duck-billed animal isn't
my mama!"
"Who is your mama, then?"
asks the kangaroo.
"She has a little round nose."
"Hmmm . . . a little round nose.
I think I know who your mama is."

Hop, hop, hop.
They stop in a field of tall grass.

MAMA?

Coco starts to cry.
"That animal looks a little like my mama, but that isn't my mama, either."
"Who is your mama, then?" asks the kangaroo.
"My mama is soft and sweet," sniffs Coco.
"Just like you?" asks the kangaroo.
"Just like me," sniffs Coco.
"Now I know who your mama is."

Hop, hop, hop. They stop at a tree.

27

And who do they see?

Not the scary
lizard,

not the busy turkey,

not the prickly
porcupine,

not the duck-billed
platypus,

not the wombat
with the little
round nose,

but **MAMA!**
Coco's very own mama!

"Come here, Coco," she says.
"I have a surprise for you."

Coco has a baby brother!